Tribal Journey

Gary Robinson

7th Generation
Summertown, Tennessee

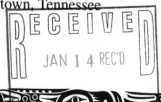

Library of Congress Cataloging-in-Publication Data

Robinson, Gary, 1950-

Tribal journey / Gary Robinson.

p. cm.

ISBN 978-1-939053-01-5 (pbk.) — ISBN 978-1-939053-87-9 (e-books)

1. Duwamish Indians--Juvenile fiction. 2. Children with disabilities--Juvenile fiction. 3. Canoes and canoeing--Juvenile fiction. 4. Self-esteem--Juvenile fiction. 5. Self-confidence--Juvenile fiction. 6. West Seattle (Seattle, Wash.)--Juvenile fiction. [1. Duwamish Indians--Fiction. 2. Indians of North America--Fiction. 3. People with disabilities--Fiction. 4. Canoes and canoeing--Fiction. 5. Self-esteem--Fiction. 6. Self-confidence--Fiction. 7. West Seattle (Seattle, Wash.)--Fiction.]

I. Title.

PZ7.R56577Tri 2013

813.6--dc23   2012044250

7th Generation, a division of
Book Publishing Company
PO Box 99, Summertown, TN 38483
888-260-8458   bookpubco.com

ISBN: 978-1-939053-01-5

18 17 16 15 14 13   1 2 3 4 5 6 7 8 9

Printed in the United States

Book Publishing Company is a member of Green Press Initiative. We chose to print this title on paper with 100% postconsumer recycled content, processed without chlorine, which saved the following natural resources:

- 16 trees
- 488 pounds of solid waste
- 7,292 gallons of water
- 1,345 pounds of greenhouse gases
- 7 million BTU of energy

green press INITIATIVE

For more information on Green Press Initiative, visit www.greenpressinitiative.org. Environmental impact estimates were made using the Environmental Defense Fund Paper Calculator. For more information visit www.papercalculator.org.

Contents

Acknowledgments. v

Chapter 1: Freedom Rings. 1

Chapter 2: Quality Family Time. 8

Chapter 3: Spring Break 21

Chapter 4: Bottomless Pit. 32

Chapter 5: Rolling Along 38

Chapter 6: Us and Them 48

Chapter 7: The Canoe Family 55

Chapter 8: Ambassadors 62

Chapter 9: Whispers on the Wind 70

Chapter 10: The Smell of the Ocean 81

Chapter 11: Crossing the Straits 86

Chapter 12: Landing Day. 95

About the Author 111

Acknowledgments

I want to thank a few people for their assistance in the development of this book.

First, there is my friend and colleague Swil Kanim, a Lummi storyteller, musician, visionary, and inspirational motivator extraordinaire. His thoughts, words, music, and prayers are always most appreciated.

Cindy Williams of the Duwamish Longhouse and Cultural Center in West Seattle graciously agreed to review the book to ensure its cultural appropriateness. It's always good to get feedback from a tribal community when creating stories and characters from that community. A big *wado* ("thank you" in Cherokee) to Cindy.

Finally, there is Jessy Lucas, who is an accomplished young Native puller, singer, and drummer, and one of the few people in the world able to play the hand flute. His work with Northwest tribal cultures, along with his own personal experiences with tribal canoe journeys, provided a solid foundation on which this book is based. His time and insights are most appreciated.

Tribal Journey

Chapter 1
Freedom Rings

I'm lucky to even be alive to tell you my story. I learned the hard way that texting and driving don't mix. And that healing can come from unexpected places. But I'm getting ahead of myself.

It was the first Friday in April. The three o'clock bell rang. Screams of joy erupted from every classroom. Spring break had arrived. Freedom at last! A whole week of unsupervised fun!

I escaped the West Seattle High School building like it was on fire.

"Jason! Jason!" I heard my name being called from across the school's front lawn. It was my best friend, Ron.

"Ron, what's up?"

"I'm jazzed," he said. "My family's spring break trip was canceled. I'll be here all next week!"

"Awesome. Maybe we can cruise the Junction. Or hit Alki Beach every day! I've got to stay in shape for the swim meet next month."

"Whoa," he said. "I don't have unlimited use of the family car, remember. I have to 'earn' it by doing chores around the house. You know, the point system."

"Oh yeah." I had to think for a minute. We were both sixteen, but neither of us had a car.

"I've got it," I said finally. "Tomorrow's Saturday. I can come over. We can work our way through a whole list of chores around your house. Maybe we can earn enough points to use the car all week."

A horn honked. We both looked to see his mom's car waiting at the curb.

"Sounds possible," Ron said. "I'll text you," he shouted, as he ran toward the car.

"Later," I shouted back.

I caught my usual bus for the ride home. Riding the bus wasn't fun, because most of the riders were younger kids. But both my parents worked, so the bus was the only way for me to get home. I usually sat in the back and looked out the window. Or just thought about stuff.

I grew up here in West Seattle. Most people don't know that this area was the original Seattle. It's where the white settlers first landed in this region to create their new home. But of course there were people already here. My mother's people—the Duwamish Indians. Her ancestors were on the shore to greet the settlers when they arrived.

Anyway, those are things I learned in the tribal culture classes my mother had me take when I was little. I'd been too busy for such things lately.

My cell phone vibrated in my pocket. I'd asked Dad for a smart phone like most of my friends had. But no luck. He said I could have one of those when I could pay for it myself.

So I flipped the lame phone open to find a text from my friend Amy Chang. "Any1 planning a get 2gether during spring break?" she asked.

I texted back, "That's what Ron & I r trying to figure out. I'll let u know."

When I became a teenager, my non-Native friends complained that Indians always lived in the past. Without much thought, I decided I agreed with them.

Of course I wanted to fit in with the other kids at school I hang out with. They're a mixture of races: whites, Asians, Latinos, blacks—you name it. Most of them had figured out how to ignore their family's past and live in the now. Track the trends. Merge with the moment.

So I decided to do likewise and go with the flow. Nothing that my Duwamish mother, grandparents, or uncles tried to teach me from Native culture really applied to life today. They were so behind the times. It was easy to turn my back on all that and go with the flow.

Another text came in. This time it was from Ben, my Latino friend. "My spring break is messed up. Got 2 go 2 Spokane 2 visit relatives."

"That sucks," I texted back. "Hope u make it thru the week—see u when u get back." I closed my phone and stuffed it back in my pocket.

What was I talking about before? Oh yeah. Going with the flow. Seattle was a great place to go with the flow. The home of Mariners baseball, Seahawks football, Starbucks coffee, and Microsoft. Sure, it was cloudy or rainy three hundred days of the year. So what. That's one of the special things about the Northwest. The weather makes everything so green.

I'd been swimming since I was little. I loved the water. I had dreams of being like Michael Phelps and winning twenty-two Olympic medals. Making the high school swim team was a step in that direction.

My cell phone vibrated again. I dug it out of my pocket one more time and flipped it open. Another text from Ron. "My mom sez chores 2moro will work fine."

I texted him back, "Hope my mom sez the same."

The bus let me out at the corner of my street. I walked the short two blocks to my house. The neighborhood was made up of little two-story brick houses that had seen better days. My house really had problems—a leaky roof, rotting front steps, and cracks in the walls.

Dad never had the time or money to fix any of this stuff. His job as a maintenance worker at the Boeing jet factory must not have paid very much. It did pay enough to keep him stocked in beer, however.

I was lucky to have my own room upstairs. It was small but all mine. It was the best place to be when Dad went on one of his rampages.

My younger brother Zak and his twin sister Shauna shared a room down the hall. Since birth they've never liked to be apart. Shauna can't sleep if Zak isn't nearby. So half of the room was filled with boy stuff, and the other half was all pink and girly.

As I approached the house, I was surprised to see my mom's car parked in the driveway.

"What are you doing home?" I asked Mom as I walked through the front door.

"It's Good Friday. Sunday is Easter. So they let some of us get off work early to have some quality family time."

That was really the last thing I was interested in.

"Can I go over to Ron's tomorrow? I told him I'd help him with a few chores."

"You? Helping with chores? Wow, that's a new one." She was smiling when she said it, so I knew she wasn't totally serious.

"We'll see. We might do something as a family. I'll talk to your father when he gets home."

I think I moaned out loud. I knew that "we'll see" was parent code for "probably not."

Chapter 2
Quality Family Time

"Absolutely not," my father said when he got home from work. "This weekend is for staying at home and being with family."

I didn't like the sound of that one bit.

"The last time we had a family weekend," I said, "you watched sports on TV while Mom refinished furniture. Shauna and Zak chased each other around the yard. I played video games in my room. What kind of quality family time is that?"

I ran up to my room before anyone could punish me for talking back. After slamming the door, I grabbed my binoculars from the dresser and focused out the window.

Since our house was on the highest hill in West Seattle, I could see pretty far in any direction. Looking west through the binoculars I could see the southern tip of Bainbridge

Island across the waters of Puget Sound. Looking east I could see freight ships carrying their loads up and down the Duwamish River. Southeast of us was the Sea-Tac Airport, with its steady stream of jets landing and taking off. Downtown Seattle, where the Space Needle is located, was just visible to the northeast.

Sometimes, when no one was around, I would sneak out of my window and onto the roof. You could see really far from there—so far that you could forget all your problems for a while.

You could forget that your father drank too much and beat Mom and us kids when he did. You could forget that your mother spent hours at the Duwamish Tribal Culture Center to escape from your father. You could forget that for some odd reason the family never had any money to do anything or fix anything or buy anything new. That was a lot to forget.

Ron texted me again. "What did they say?"

"They said no," was all I replied and closed the phone. What was I to do now? I could grit my teeth and try to get through another day. As usual.

Instead, I decided to send a text blast to all my friends to let them know what was going on. Maybe someone would have an idea for how I could get out of the Saturday family time. So I started thumb-typing.

"Guys, I need your help. How can I get out of spending the entire weekend with my lame family? Got ideas?" I pushed the send button and hoped.

Within minutes reply messages came back from Ron, Amy, Ben, and Randy. Ashley must not have had her phone handy.

"U can always sneak out in the middle of the nite," Ben suggested.

"Tell ur parents my auntie died and u hav 2 come 2 comfort me," Amy replied. Her message ended with a smiley face. I think she wants to be more than friends. I'm not ready.

"Put sleeping pills in their breakfast so they fall asleep. They won't know u left until it's 2 late," Ron offered.

"Tell em ur sick & need 2 lie down," Randy's text began. "Go 2 ur room & close the door. Fix ur bed 2 look like u r asleep under the covers. Then sneak out. I saw this in a movie."

Wow. These all sounded like terrible ideas. I'm not a very good liar.

Then Ashley's text came in. "Honesty is the best policy," her message said. "Ask for a family meeting. Tell your parents how you feel and why. Even if you don't get what you want, it will bring the family closer. Talking it out is always a good thing."

That seemed like the worst idea yet. Ashley didn't really fit in with the rest of the crowd. And her message was so proper. Everything was spelled out completely and correctly with no text shortcuts. Well, she did like to read a lot. And she always said she was going to be a writer when she grew up. I had to remember not to include her in future text blasts.

"Jason!" My mother's voice echoed up the stairs. "Time to come down for dinner."

As I sat down at the table, my cell phone vibrated. I took it out of my pocket to see who was texting me. My father immediately grabbed the phone from my hand and put it next to his plate.

"New rule," he said. "No texting at the dinner table."

"But I—" That's all I could say before Dad interrupted.

"You're on that thing too much. Breakfast, lunch, and dinner are times for us to focus on being right here. At work they said lots of parents are doing this now."

I remained silent and began eating. The room was quiet except for the sound of forks scraping on plates.

Later, I asked about the family's plans for this Saturday.

"You'll find out tomorrow," my dad barked and took a sip of his beer. He jerked in the middle of the sip. I could tell that Mom had kicked him under the table.

"Your father and I haven't had any time to talk about it, but we will tonight," Mom said softly.

"Why don't we all get a chance to say what we want to do?" I asked. I don't even know where that came from. It just jumped out of my mouth.

"You kids aren't smart enough to—" Dad began. He jerked again. "Ow," he said, and reached down to rub his leg.

"Watch yourself, woman," he snarled at Mom.

"Actually, Jason, since you're sixteen, I do think you're old enough to have a vote," Mom said. "What would you like to do?"

"I was thinking that Sunday might be a better day for family time. It *is* Easter and all. I think there's a spring street fair at the Junction. We could all go and check it out."

I held my breath. How would they react?

"You mean after church, right, Jason?" Mom asked.

"Of course." Actually I'd forgotten about church. Christmas, Easter, and All Saints

Day were the only times we went. That was Dad's rule.

"That's not a bad idea," Mom said. "What do you think, Jack?"

"You and I will talk about this later," Dad said through clenched teeth. "Right now, let's finish eating."

That was the end of the conversation. Wow. We actually almost had a family meeting like Ashley had suggested.

Dad usually didn't like talking about things. He just barked commands at us. He came from a loud German-American family. Family reunions with them were kind of weird. All they did was drink beer and complain.

A lot of people think all Indians are alcoholics. Not in my family.

When dinner was over I grabbed my phone off the table and headed up to my room. It was still light outside, thanks to daylight saving time. What a cool invention. Everyone agrees to set their clocks ahead an hour this time of year. Then, magically, there's an extra hour of sunlight at the end of the day for the spring and summer.

I picked up my binoculars and ear buds. Opening my bedroom window, I climbed out onto the roof. I had to take each step carefully on the slanted cedar tiles.

I made my way over to the west side of the house. It had been a rare sunny day in the Pacific Northwest. The sun reflected brightly off the water in the distance. It shimmered like gold in the light.

I could tell from the sun's position low in the sky that it would be setting in about an hour. I liked to watch it go down. I put the ear buds in and started the playlist on my phone. I texted Ron.

"There's a chance I could make it 2moro. Parents r talking about doing the family thing on Sunday."

He replied without delay.

"Great. Keep me posted."

I leaned back, listened to the music, and relaxed. I knew there'd be some fireworks later inside the house when my parents talked about my Sunday family idea. But I wasn't going to worry about that now. I shut off my mind and focused on the music. In a few minutes I nodded off to sleep.

When I woke up, the sun was just sliding down beyond Bainbridge Island. I imagined it settling into the water like someone taking a bath. The air was becoming cooler. I decided to go back inside.

As I climbed in and closed the window I heard loud voices from downstairs. The fireworks had already started. I couldn't make out what words they were saying, or rather yelling, at each other. I could tell they were angry words. Dad must really be drunk.

Then he screamed something that I could understand.

"You whacked-out squaw! I should've never got mixed up with you!"

Then came a loud crash, like a glass being thrown against the wall. That was followed by the sound of large furniture being overturned. Mom let loose a fearful yell. That was it.

I ran out of the room and down the hall to check on Zak and Shauna. They were in their room with the door closed. I opened it and looked in on them. They were watching their *Finding Nemo* DVD for the hundredth time.

"We heard yelling," Zak said. "What's going on?"

"I'm going to find out. Stay here and keep watching your video." I closed the door and took the stairs three at a time.

When I got to the kitchen, I found Mom on the floor moaning. My father was standing over her. A shattered glass lay beside her. The kitchen table was on its side.

"You sorry excuse for a father!" I screamed as I ran full force at Dad. I hit him in the stomach with my head and knocked him against the cabinet. He hit it with a thwack. Then he bounced off the cabinet and landed on the floor across the room from Mom. He must've passed out from too much alcohol, because he didn't move.

I stood and looked down at this man who had tortured us for years.

"You're never going to hurt Mom again, do you hear me?"

I kneeled down beside Mom. A red knot was forming on her cheek where Dad had hit her. Her chin was bleeding. She seemed a little dazed.

"Come on," I said. "We've got to get out of here."

I helped her to her feet. Then I slung her arm over my shoulder. We walked toward the living room. I pulled the car keys off the hook where Mom kept them and headed for the front door.

"But what about Zak and Shauna?" she said weakly.

"I'll put you in the car and then go up and get them."

"Where are we going?" Mom asked.

"First to the hospital emergency room to have you checked out. I'll figure something out after that."

Mom nodded and allowed me to lead her to the minivan. I put Zak and Shauna in next. They were scared and confused. As I drove to the West Seattle Hospital a couple of miles away, I explained what was going on.

After helping Mom get into an examination room, I returned to the waiting room to watch my brother and sister. They found some toys and children's books to keep them busy. I texted Ron.

"Call me as soon as possible. Emergency!"

In a few minutes my phone rang.

"What's up?" Ron asked when we got connected.

"There's been a major disaster at my house. Mom and Dad got into it. Mom was hurt. So I drove us to the ER, where we are now. Zak and Shauna are with me."

"That's radical, dude!"

"Ron, this is serious. We need a place to stay for the night. Away from my dad. Do you think your parents would let us spend the night?"

"I don't see why not. Let me talk to them. I'll call you back."

I closed my phone and felt very tired. I closed my eyes and felt the emotional impact of what had happened.

What a hard, crazy night. So much for quality family time.

Chapter 3
Spring Break

Ron's mother called a short while later. She said they'd be happy for us to spend the night at their house. So after the hospital finished treating Mom, I drove us to Ron's house.

"Irene, I'm sorry to hear of your troubles," Ron's mom told my mom.

"We're so grateful for your hospitality," Mom said.

"We've got a spare bedroom upstairs that you and your little ones can share. Jason can bunk with Ron in his room."

We settled in for the night. As I lay trying to fall asleep, my mind replayed those horrible images. My father standing over my bleeding mother. The anger that boiled over in me. My physical attack on Dad. Us escaping into the night. Only after we had left the house did fear creep into my thoughts.

And that's the last thing I remember before nodding off.

The next morning, right after breakfast, Mom gathered us kids together for a private family meeting.

"There's a place called the Chief Seattle Family Center not too far from here," she said. "They have rooms for families in situations like ours. I'm going to apply for us to move in there for a while."

"But what about our toys and clothes?" Shauna asked with a worried look.

"And all our DVDs and video games?" Zak added.

"We'll pick up those things one day while your father is at work."

That seemed to satisfy them—for now.

"Since we're here, can I help Ron with those chores I asked you about?" I said.

"Tell me again why you want to help him with his chores?" Mom was suspicious.

"Well, we want to use his mom's car to visit friends and go to the beach and do stuff during spring break. He has to earn points to use her car."

"I see," Mom said. "Okay, I guess. As a matter of fact, we can all help Ron's mom and dad with chores to repay them for letting us stay."

The first thing Ron and I did was clean the garage. We took everything out and put the stuff in the driveway. Bikes, tools, lawn mower, storage boxes—the usual garage stuff. Then we hosed down the floor and brushed it with soapy water. While the floor dried we moved on down the list of chores. We finished the list by lunchtime. Yay!

During lunch Mom reported that she had called the family center. A family had just moved out, so they would have space for us Monday afternoon. Another yay! So the plan was for us to go home late Monday morning after Dad left for work and get whatever we needed.

In the meantime, we enjoyed being with Ron's family for the weekend.

At about eleven o'clock Monday morning, Mom drove Zak, Shauna, and me back to our house. We made sure Dad's car was gone before parking in the driveway.

"Okay, let's do this quickly," Mom said. "We don't want to be here when your father comes home. Each of you grab a suitcase for clothes and a box for other things. That's all the room we'll have at the center."

We went inside and gathered the things each of us thought were most important. I took my binoculars, skateboard, swimsuit, and summer clothes.

Zak filled his suitcase and box only with toys, games, and DVDs. So he had to go back upstairs and dump half of that stuff to make room for clothes.

Shauna did exactly what Mom had asked, bringing down a collection of her stuff. It was all neatly folded, stacked, and arranged.

Mom had to pick up extra things like her checkbook, wallet, and some important papers. As we were driving to the center, she said she'd need those as we started living on our own.

"What do you mean 'start living on our own?'" I asked. "Aren't we going to move back to our house after you and Dad work things out?" She pulled the car over near a park with a playground and turned off the engine. We all got out.

"Zak and Shauna, why don't you go over and play on the swings or the slide while I talk to your brother," Mom said.

The pair happily raced to the slide to see who would go on it first. Mom and I sat down at a picnic table.

"Jason, what you did for us the other night was very brave. I am really proud of you." I blushed a little. "Your father and his drinking and fighting have only gotten worse over the years. I've begged him to get help, but he refuses. So, thanks to you, I've finally gotten up the nerve to get us away from him— for good."

I was confused.

"You mean we have to stay in the shelter forever?"

"No, just for a while. Until I can make other arrangements for us and end things with your father."

"Divorce?"

"Yes, I'm afraid so. But you, me, Zak, and Shauna will be together. And the shelter will help us find a home we can afford. Your father will still be your father. When I'm sure he's not going to hurt any of us, then we'll arrange visits. Okay?"

"Okay," I said. Mom was right. We had to be away from Dad for a while.

So we drove to the shelter and moved our stuff in, what little we had. The people who ran the Chief Seattle Family Center were very nice. They said a school bus picked up and dropped off kids there every day. Though our room was small, there was a nice shaded play area out back. There also was a library with a study area for doing homework.

Mom tried her best to get us three kids to look at the bright side of it all. "Be brave and hopeful," she said. I was trying to do that, and so was Shauna.

But Zak was the least convinced. He just knew we were going to end up living out on the street someday soon. In a cardboard box.

As I arranged my little corner of the room, Ron texted me. "How's the new place?"

"Small & depressing, but it will have 2 do for now," I replied. "When can we get the gang 2gether & go 2 the beach? I need a change of scenery and a swim."

"2moro at noon," Ron shot back. "Send me ur address so I can pick u up."

"All rite. Now ur talking!" I sent him the address and told Mom about the plan. She was fine with it. I was relieved.

Noon the next day took forever to get here. When Ron arrived, I ran out to the car carrying my towel and swimsuit. My mom had given me a little spending money for lunch and snacks, so we were good to go.

Technically, in Washington State, sixteen-year-olds weren't supposed to drive other sixteen-year-olds unless they were related.

Ron's parents were sort of relaxed about those rules. Especially since his mom and dad both worked, and Ron often drove his brother to school.

"We're picking up Ben and Amy," Ron explained. "Randy's meeting us at Alki."

"Awesome!" I said. "How long do we have the car?"

"I have to be home by six o'clock sharp for dinner."

"That gives us six whole hours. Let's make the most of it. We're lucky it's another sunny day."

Alki Beach was really the only beach in the area. People from all over Seattle showed up there to hike, bike, roller-skate, and just soak up the sun, if there was any. The water was too cold for most people to swim in, but not me. Usually I dived in, swam like crazy for a few minutes, and then rapidly retreated to the warmth of a towel.

We did almost everything there was to do at Alki, including having lunch at the Beachside Cafe. That's where we hatched our plan to have a bonfire on the beach Sunday night. That would be our last night of freedom on spring break before we had to head back to school.

The rest of the week went by smoothly, though I really didn't get a chance to do enough swimming. But I could hardly wait until Friday. Mom said I was very helpful all week, so she decided I could use her car to go to the bonfire. Yay! That doesn't happen very often. My parents were stricter than Ron's about sixteen-year-olds driving other kids around. But Mom said it couldn't hurt this one time.

Ron would ride with me, since his house was on the way to the beach. Everyone else would meet us there.

At about six o'clock on Friday, I told Mom good-bye and left the family shelter. I had a little money in my pocket and my cell phone on the car's center console. In the back seat were all the fixings for s'mores, thanks to Mom. And in the trunk was some firewood I had gathered during the week. Everything was set.

I was headed north on California Avenue. The traffic was a little heavy. It was Friday at 6:00 p.m., after all. Rush hour. After a few blocks, the traffic stopped moving completely. What was up?

I put the car in park and stepped out on the pavement for a look ahead. Road construction. Orange signs read "Road Work Ahead" and "Flagman Ahead. Be Prepared to Stop."

Just great. I sat back down in the car and picked up my phone. "Stuck in traffic," I texted Ron. "Don't know how long. I'll let u know when I'm moving again."

"No sweat," he responded. "See u when u get here."

After fifteen minutes, traffic began flowing again. It was still thick and slow. When I got up alongside the construction site, I could see they'd finished working for the day. So I pushed on as fast as I could. There was fun to get to!

Soon I was passing through the Junction, the old downtown part of West Seattle. At the intersection of California Avenue and Oregon Street, my phone alerted me to another text. I looked down at the phone in my lap to see who it was from. It was Ron.

That's when it came. Out of nowhere. BAM! In the split second that I was distracted, the light in my lane had changed from green to yellow to red. To my left, a driver in a hurry jumped from the line when his light turned green. I hadn't cleared the intersection.

My car was hit from the left side, the driver's side—my side. The other driver must've been distracted, too.

Crash! Bang! Crunch! My car flipped on its right side. In an instant I was hanging sideways from the seatbelt as the car slid on its side across the pavement. Slam! Directly into a corner light pole. All I could feel was sharp, burning pain up and down the left side of my body. Then I blacked out.

Chapter 4
Bottomless Pit

I don't know how long I was out. When I woke up, I found myself in a strange room, in a strange bed. I had trouble opening my eyes. When I finally got them open, I didn't like what I saw.

I was in a hospital room. There were machines beside my bed. They were beeping and making weird noises. I had a headache and a side ache and an arm ache. But I couldn't feel my left leg.

I looked down at it. The whole leg, from my toes to my hip, was in a thick white cast. What was going on? What had happened? My mind was in a fog.

Slowly I looked around the room. There was Mom asleep in a chair next to the bed.

"Mom? Mom, what happened?" She woke up and looked at me.

"Oh, Jason. I'm so glad you're awake. Don't try to talk. I'll call the doctor to come check you."

"What happened to me?"

"Don't you remember? You were in a terrible car wreck. Two days ago." As Mom left to find the doctor, the images of the accident flooded back into my mind. That made the throbbing pain in various parts of my body return. I moaned.

My first thought was that I missed the beach bonfire with all of my friends. How terrible was that!

The next few days were a blur. I slept a lot—when I wasn't being poked, prodded, and probed by various doctors and nurses. They'd examine me and then go off to a corner of the room and talk to each other in whispers. None of them looked very happy.

Finally one of the doctors came into the room with my mother.

"Son, the doctor has some news to tell us," she said, and then stepped back.

The doctor, an old man with white hair and wire-rimmed glasses, moved in close to the bed.

"Jason, I'm just going to give it to you straight," he said. "We think you may not be able to use your left leg again."

"How long will that be?" I asked.

"As far as we can tell right now, forever," he replied. He paused for a moment to let that sink into my brain. "There was damage to your spine where the nerves from your leg connect to your central nervous system."

I thought I understood what he was saying. But I didn't like it at all. I was too shocked to speak. Mom was crying as she rushed around to the other side of my bed. She bent down to hug me.

"It may take weeks before you can get yourself around in a wheelchair," he went on to say. "Maybe months. It all depends on you and how much you actively take part in your own recovery."

He went on talking, but I couldn't hear what he was saying. It all became too depressing. I felt like I was moving through a tunnel away from Mom, the doctor, and the hospital room. Then the tunnel became a dark hole. I landed at the bottom of it. I think I passed out.

As the days went by, I found out more about the accident. A nineteen-year-old girl was driving the car that hit me. She was texting as she drove through that intersection. And she walked away from the accident with only a few cuts and bruises. How fair was that?

"I blame myself," Mom said. "I'm the one who let you drive the car."

"Don't go there, Mom," I said. "I'm the one who wasn't paying attention."

For days Mom regularly tried to cheer me up. So did Zak and Shauna when they came to visit.

My friends came by to see me, too. They all said they were so sorry about what happened to me. It sort of sounded like they were talking to me through a tin can attached to a string. I really couldn't connect to them. They talked for a few minutes until they ran out of things to say. Then they left. And I was alone again.

Mom brought schoolwork for me to do so I wouldn't fall behind. But I didn't care. I wasn't interested in doing schoolwork. I wasn't interested in anything.

The nurses must have started giving me some new medicine. In a few days I didn't feel like I was in a hole any more. I still felt sort of numb, but the hole was fading away.

About a month after the accident, Mom came to my room one morning with a big smile on her face. She said, "Jason, you get to go home tomorrow. What do you think about that?"

"Depends. Do you mean the shelter or our actual home?"

"I mean our actual home. Soon after your accident I filed for divorce from your father."

"You actually did it," I said.

"Yes," Mom said. "And the judge issued a special order that says your father can't come near any of us until he gets treatment for his problems."

"Is that why Dad hasn't tried to see me?" I asked. "I mean—I know I'm mad at him and all. And I'm not ready to forgive him. But he's still my dad."

"It's complicated," Mom replied. "He asked how you were doing. But we can talk about that another time. For now, your father has moved out of the house so you could be in your own home to recover."

"That sounds pretty good," I said.

"Your father also agreed to go to counseling to get help with his drinking and his violent behavior. He may be ready for a visit in a few weeks."

"We'll see how I feel about it when the time comes," I replied.

The next day the doctor took off my big thick cast and replaced it with a thinner, lighter one. Afterward, the nurse rolled a wheelchair into the room. With Mom's help I got into it.

"Let's go home," Mom said.

"Let's go home," I said.

Chapter 5
Rolling Along

There had been some changes made to the house. Workmen from the Chief Seattle Center had built a wheelchair ramp up to the front door.

Mom pushed me up the ramp and into the house. It felt so good to be back there even though the memory of the night we left was still in the air. Mom had moved everything from my upstairs room down to her old bedroom so I could roll right in.

The next day a Mrs. Anderson came from the hospital to talk to me. She told me that she was the hospital's physical therapist.

"What's a physical therapist?" I asked.

"I figure out a plan for your physical recovery," she said. "I know exactly what body movements you need to start doing to help you get your strength back. And they will also help your muscles, joints, and bones heal."

"What's the point? I'm never going to walk again. Or swim. I'll forever be the kid in the wheelchair."

"That's only true if you believe it to be true," she said. "Your own belief in yourself can make a big difference in the outcome."

She explained how the physical therapy process worked. She also told me how long it might take to see results. It all sounded pretty pointless to me. I guess she was used to dealing with people like me. People who felt like giving up before they even started.

"When your cast comes off, I'll bring you a crutch to use," she continued. "Your right leg is still good. You won't have to spend all your time in a wheelchair."

"What a choice," I said. "The crutch or the wheelchair." She ignored my sarcasm.

Before leaving, she told me, "We'll start physical therapy next week, whether you want to or not. Your mother has already signed the forms."

Won't that be fun, I thought.

A few days later—I think it was the middle of May—Mom brought an older Native American man to see me. He kind of looked like someone I may have met a long time ago at one of the tribal culture classes I went to. He had brown wrinkly skin, two braids of grey hair, and a look on his face that made it seem like he knew a secret nobody else knew.

Mom said, "Jason, I don't know if you remember Mr. Franks. He's come to visit you."

The man approached my bed and reached out his hand to shake. I didn't move. Mom continued, "Mr. Franks is working with the tribal youth at the Duwamish Cultural Center, teaching them our language, songs, and dances."

"That's nice," I said. "Didn't my mother tell you I wouldn't be dancing ever again?"

"Jason, don't be rude!" Mom said firmly.

Mr. Franks signaled Mom that it was all right. He pulled up a chair next to the bed and sat down facing me. Without saying a word, he reached out his hand again, this time palm up. He was inviting me to put my hand in his. I was curious, so I did.

He put his other hand on top of mine and looked into my eyes for what seemed like forever. A song began to rise from somewhere inside him. First it was a humming. Then Indian words started forming. The sound was low and kind of calming. He closed his eyes and the song filled the room. In a few moments I closed my eyes, too.

I must have fallen asleep or passed out, because in a few minutes I opened my eyes and saw that Mr. Franks was no longer in my room. The singing had stopped. I could hear him talking softly to Mom out in the living room.

In a minute they both came back into my room.

"What just happened?" I asked.

Mr. Franks spoke to me for the first time. "Your soul has been very far away from your body. I called it to come back to be with you again. You should start feeling better about things now."

That sounded kind of crazy. I looked to Mom to see if I could tell what she thought about it.

She said, "Mr. Franks and I think it would be good for you to start sitting in on the tribal culture classes. It would help for you to be around our people more and learn about that part of yourself again. It would be healing."

"Okay," I said without thinking. Wait. Why did I say that? That's not what I intended to say. What was going on with me?

"See you next Saturday," Mr. Franks said with a smile. He shook hands with me and my mother and left.

The next day Mom rolled me and my wheelchair into the back of the minivan. She'd had some changes made so the wheelchair could easily fit in the side door. There were also clamps in the floor that held the chair. That way it wouldn't roll around as she drove.

She took me to the hospital so the doctor could take off my cast. Even with the cast off, there was no feeling in my left leg. It was dead. I had to pick it up with both hands to move it.

As promised, Mrs. Anderson brought me a crutch made of aluminum. It was the kind that could be folded up when not being used. It could fit in the pocket on the back of the wheelchair. Whoopee-do. I was less than excited about it all.

I started physical therapy sessions the very next day. Mrs. Anderson said I needed daily physical activity or my muscles would just quit working. She showed me how to do exercises at home that would make me stronger and improve my balance.

What she wanted me to do was hard. But I was so bored I decided to give it a try. I thought I'd just go with the flow like before.

By the time next Saturday came I was definitely having second—and third and fourth—thoughts about going to the tribal culture class. In fact, I wasn't sure about it at all. But I had promised my mother, so I went.

The Duwamish Longhouse sat across the street from the Duwamish River. They said that a long time ago the river was beautiful, with a natural shoreline. Now it was like a big open water pipe lined with cement borders and boat docks. Freight barges moved up and down the river carrying loads in and out of the factories and warehouses in the area.

The Longhouse was near the only natural shoreline that was left. I had learned that this was part of the traditional Duwamish homeland. This was where Chief Seattle had lived. He was the man the city had been named after. So here his people had stayed.

The language class had already started when I arrived. It was being held in a classroom on the second floor. The room was lined with windows that looked out on the river. A dozen or so teens sat on folding chairs in a circle around Mr. Franks. He was talking Indian to them. A few elderly women sat nearby listening.

I'm glad I'd learned how to get around in my wheelchair on my own so Mom didn't have to come in with me. How embarrassing would that have been?

Mr. Franks paused when he saw me. "Jason, I'm glad you could make it. Come join the circle."

I wheeled over as a couple of the kids scooted sideways to make room for me.

"Everyone, this is Jason," Mr. Franks said. "Jason, this is everyone." They all said "hi" or "hello" or something in the tribal language I didn't understand.

I listened to what was going on for a while, but it really didn't catch my attention. Mr. Franks said the Salish people lived in villages up and down the coast of Washington. The language used by tribes in the area was called Lushootseed. I couldn't even pronounce the name of the language, much less words from the language.

He had everyone in the circle practice saying a few tribal words. We were to then use those words in a song he taught us.

But all the while, I could hear noises coming from outside that sounded like a chain saw cutting into wood. When we took a break from the language lesson, I wheeled over to the windows and pulled myself up out of the chair. Leaning on the windowsill, I peered outside.

Down below, across the street and closer to the river, a man was cutting into a huge cedar tree that lay on the ground. He was shaping it into what I thought could only be a very large canoe. A couple of other younger men were helping him. They used some kind of tool that was shaped like an axe to hack away at the inside of the tree. It looked like they were trying to hollow it out.

"What are they doing down there?" I asked Mr. Franks.

"They're carving a dugout canoe," he said. "It will be used this summer to paddle up to a tribal community in Canada. It's part of the yearly canoe journey that all the Coast Salish tribes take part in."

I continued to watch the men work on the massive tree. Something about it drew my attention. I couldn't take my eyes off it. Mr. Franks must've noticed.

"Jason, do you want to come back and join the circle now?" he asked. "Or would you rather go outside to watch them carve?"

I was so focused on the canoe I guess I didn't hear him. He knelt down beside my wheelchair and looked down at the carvers.

"Jason, you've just given me an idea." He turned back to the class. "We're all going to go with Jason down to the canoe to continue our class. Who wants to help him with his chair?"

Chapter 6
Us and Them

When we all got down to the carving site, Mr. Franks spoke privately to the carver for a few minutes. Then he turned to us.

"This is Billy James. He's a master carver who's come down from Canada to carve a canoe that can go on the ocean. It will be used for our tribe so we can participate in the tribal canoe journey this year. He's going to explain a little about what he's doing. Then we can watch him work."

The carver told us that Native people of this area used red cedar trees that were more than three hundred years old to make canoes. He also explained about the traditional tools used for carving.

"Today, carvers use chain saws and steel tools for creating canoes and totem poles. Our ancestors would've used those too if they'd been available."

He fired up the chain saw and finished shaping the front of the canoe. He roughed out a fairly sharp point that tilted upward. He said the front was called the bow.

His two assistants moved back to the sides of the log. They began removing more wood from the inside center of the log with their hand tools. They chipped away at the cedar one little piece at a time. It looked like it would take a year to finish.

As we watched them work, Mr. Franks said, "They'll be finished with this canoe within a month."

A month? How was that possible?

"Until it's completed, we've borrowed another canoe to practice with," he continued.

"Practice what?" I asked.

"Practice pulling, so we'll be ready for the Tribal Journey in July," one of the older kids said.

"Pulling? What's pulling?"

"Paddling the canoe," the boy answered. "But it's called pulling because you pull the paddle through the water to make the canoe go forward."

"How come you guys know so much about this?" I asked.

"Because we're all part of the canoe family, and we'll all be pulling this year," another kid replied.

"You have got to be joking," I said in disbelief. "Your parents are going to let you paddle to Canada?"

"That's why we're learning the language and the songs," one of the girls in the class added. "It's all part of learning the ancient canoe culture."

Billy James picked up one of the hand tools near the canoe. He brought it with him as he walked toward me. He held it out to me, and I took it from him.

"This is called an adze," he said.

I looked at it closely. It had a flat, wide metal blade with a short wooden handle.

"Traditionally, our carvers used ones made from stone," he went on. "This one's made of steel. If you'd like, you can come over and see how it feels to carve a canoe."

He couldn't be serious, could he?

"No thanks," I said holding the adze out for him to take. "I really can't do much of anything anymore."

"Mr. Franks said you could do almost anything if you really want to," Billy replied. "But that's all right. You think about it." He left the tool with me. I felt the weight of the adze in my hands for a moment before putting it down.

The next day I went to the physical therapy clinic to work with Mrs. Anderson. As in every session, she had me up out of my chair. I was holding on to two parallel bars as I struggled to sort of walk. It was more like a shuffle really. I wasn't very good at it, but she said it was important for me to make the effort.

"You must never give up," she said.

Next she showed me a new way to use my crutch to pull myself out of the wheelchair and onto a bed. She pointed out that this was one of the reasons I needed to be doing exercises. I had to build my upper body strength.

I decided to tell her about my experience with the tribal culture class and the canoe carver's offer.

"Do you really think I could actually work on carving that canoe?" I asked.

She thought for a moment.

"It sounds like the ideal exercise to build your arm and shoulder muscles," she said. "Especially if you switch off every fifteen minutes or so. Chop with the adze using your right arm for a while. Then turn around so you can chop with your left arm for a while."

And that's what I did. On Mondays, Wednesdays, and Fridays, I worked with Mrs. Anderson. And on Tuesdays, Thursdays, and Saturdays, I worked with Billy carving the canoe.

Billy taught me a lot about the canoes and the people who made them. The Duwamish tribe was one of many Salish tribes in the area who shared an ancient canoe culture. He said the water was their highway. They made several different kinds of canoes for different jobs.

One day, when we had taken a break from carving, Billy looked at me and got all serious. He said, "Jason, this canoe is part of who you are. When we talk about what your ancestors did, it would be normal for you to say 'we' instead of 'they,' and 'our' instead of 'their.'"

I didn't get what he was saying. He noticed my puzzled look.

"The water was *our* highway, not *their* highway. *We* made different kinds of canoes for traveling and hauling and fishing. Do you understand the difference? You need to own this. You need to claim it. Then it will truly become a part of you and give you strength."

It was like a light turned on in my head. I got it. It meant I belonged here to these people. This was a part of my life. It meant I could no longer pretend I wasn't Indian. And when I accepted that, a new feeling flooded into me. It was a feeling of pride. A feeling of ease.

I began right then to accept myself for who I am. I stepped across the line between *me* and *them* and became part of the *we*.

Chapter 7
The Canoe Family

That's when the dream started. Every night for a week I'd see the same thing in my sleep.

I was walking through a forest near a clear running stream. Tall, majestic cedar trees stood all around me. A woodpecker in one nearby tree was tap-tap-tapping on the tree's trunk. He tapped so hard the tree fell over and landed in the stream. I walked over to look at the fallen tree.

A large black bird, a raven, flew down and landed on the tree. That's when he spoke to me. And that's when I always woke up. But I never could remember what the raven said. Finally I told my mom about the dream. She said she'd speak to Mr. Franks about it.

"Why Mr. Franks?" I asked.

"Because he's a wise man," she said. "He knows about such things."

The following Saturday a large crowd of people of all ages gathered at the canoe. The class members were there, but I didn't know the rest of them. Everyone seemed to know who I was though.

"Who are all these people?" I asked Billy, who stood near the canoe.

"The canoe family," he answered. "You'll find out in a minute what this is about. Stay up here with me."

Mr. Franks stepped up to the canoe's bow. He began singing a prayer song. The crowd grew quiet. The song was similar to the one he sang the first day I met him.

When he finished he said, "I've called this meeting of our canoe family for a couple of reasons. Billy, you go first."

"I've been watching for a sign that would tell me what name this canoe would go by," Billy said. "You know, every Salish canoe has a spirit. That spirit speaks to those who create the canoe and use it. I'm happy to say we have the name."

Then Mr. Franks spoke again.

"I want you all to meet Jason Morgan," he said as he put a hand on my shoulder. "You've no doubt heard about him, his terrible accident, and the contribution he's been making as a carver."

People in the crowd nodded. Some spoke a few words in their—our—native language.

"Jason is the one who has given us the name for our canoe," he added.

No one was more shocked to hear that than me. What was he talking about?

"Jason dreamed the dream given by the cedar tree spirit guide, the woodpecker," he continued.

"In his dream, the raven flew down and landed on the cedar tree. Thus the spirit of Raven gave his permission and his blessing on the canoe. So from this moment forward our canoe is the Raven Canoe. And we are the Raven Canoe Family. We'll have a canoe-naming ceremony when the carving is complete."

I certainly wasn't expecting this. They gathered around me and congratulated me.

Everyone in the group raised their hands, palms up, moving them up and down. This was the traditional Salish gesture of thanks that I'd seen as a child.

They were all so happy. I was surprised and happy too. I wasn't sure what it all meant, but I realized it was still good to go with the flow.

"And there's more," Mr. Franks said. We all quieted down. "I've spoken to Jason's mother and his physical therapist."

Mr. Franks knew my physical therapist? How'd that happen? What's been going on behind my back?

"Jason, we are formally inviting you to join our Tribal Journey this year. We want you to pull with us next month when we paddle to the shores of the Cowichan people in Canada."

"I—I don't know what to say," I stammered. "This is all so sudden."

The image of my wheelchair flashed in my mind.

"How could that even work?" I asked. "I mostly live in a wheelchair."

"Our practice canoe is over at the river's edge," Mr. Franks responded. "We'll show you just how that will work."

He nodded to Billy. The master carver grabbed my wheelchair handles and pushed me toward the river. Everyone followed. When we reached the shoreline, two of the adults stood knee-deep in the water and steadied the canoe.

Billy picked me up in his arms and carried me. He waded into the water beside the canoe. Then he gently set me down on one of the canoe's crossbeam seats. There was already a cushion on the seat waiting for me.

Six kids and young adults climbed in next, filling the canoe's middle section. They picked up the paddles that had been stowed in the canoe. As they passed them out, the young man closest to me handed me one. There was an image of a raven on the widest part of the paddle.

"I'm Jessy," the young man said. He had a scraggly mustache and a long dark ponytail down to the middle of his back. We shook hands.

Next, Billy climbed into the back seat in the canoe's stern. He steered the canoe around so the bow nudged the shore. To my surprise, Mr. Franks climbed in the canoe's front seat and picked up the last paddle.

"What's Mr. Franks doing in the canoe?" I asked.

"You didn't know?" Jessy said. "He's the head of this whole canoe family and our main skipper."

"Is there anything he *doesn't* do?" I asked.

"He's a terrible cook," Jessy said, and laughed as the canoe moved out into the river.

And so it began. I switched from carving to pulling. I was on the water again. Not in it, but the next best thing. I could tell that my muscles had grown stronger from the carving.

Now they'd grow even stronger from using that raven paddle.

At one of the practices, Mr. Franks presented me with a traditional Salish hat made of woven strips of cedar bark. He told me it was a gift from the canoe family. He said that it would come in handy to keep the sun out of my face out on the open water. I'd seen others wearing such a hat. Having my own made me feel an even stronger sense of pride.

It all felt so right. Why had I avoided my Nativeness all this time? Because it didn't seem cool? This was by far the coolest thing I'd ever been involved in.

Chapter 8
Ambassadors

At first Mom wouldn't hear of it. She didn't want me taking part in the journey or spending any time in the canoe out on the water. What if the boat flipped over? I couldn't swim anymore. I'd probably drown.

"First of all," I said, "we never call the canoe a boat, out of respect for the canoe traditions. I'd get thrown overboard for sure if I called it a boat. Second, this was all Mr. Franks's idea. You said he was a wise man, so I think we should do what he says. Third, I need to do this. I don't know why, but I feel like there's something here I need to be part of."

I kept talking and explaining and pleading. I told her the canoe family had promised to take care of me and make sure I didn't fall out of the canoe. Finally, she understood how important this was to me. She changed her mind and signed the permission form that allowed me to participate.

"You never could do just a little bit of something," she said. "You always had to go all the way. Jump in with both feet. I hope you know what you're doing."

"So do I," I said with a big sigh.

I quickly learned there were lots of rules for canoeing. And there were guidelines for pulling on the ocean. These were serious rules to keep paddlers safe during the long hours spent on the rough waters.

Everyone else had been learning the rules and practicing with the canoe for months. I had to take a crash course, because our paddle to Cowichan began in two weeks.

I trained every day so I'd be ready for the two-hundred-mile trip. Practice sessions were held at one of my favorite places: Alki Beach.

Jessy became my closest brother within the Raven Canoe Family. He'd been on last year's Tribal Journey and knew how things worked.

"Out on the open water, your life jacket is your best friend," he said. "If you wear it and the canoe capsizes, it will save your life."

He handed me one. I put it on and tightened the straps. It felt a little awkward. I fiddled with it trying to make it more comfortable.

"Some people would rather sit on theirs instead of wearing it. But last year they told us we could sit on it only if we wanted to be comfortable *right before we drowned.*"

Ha-ha, very funny, I thought.

There were so many things I had to do over and over again until I could do them without thinking. Like matching my paddle stroke to the person's in front of me. Like pulling my paddle out of the water and holding it straight up when we were cruising. Like learning all the signals that pullers used to communicate clearly and quickly out on the water.

We even had to practice flipping the canoe over—with us *in it*—so we'd know how to survive in the freezing-cold ocean. Our canoe trainer, a Native guy named Joseph, had been on several canoe journeys and ran a kayak rental company. He said that if we were in the cold water too long our brains and muscles would quit working and we'd pass out.

"I'm used to the cold water," I told Joseph just before he flipped the canoe. "I used to swim here at Alki Beach at least once a week."

"That's great, Jason," he replied. "That probably means you'll turn blue fifteen minutes after everyone else does."

I thought maybe he was kidding around, but I wasn't sure. He was wearing a wet suit that covered him from the neck down so he was warm. He stood waist-deep in the water next to our canoe. His assistant stood on the other side, also wearing a wet suit.

"The canoe will float no matter what," Joseph told our group. "So, when it rolls over, hang on to it or climb on top of it until you're rescued."

At the count of three, Joseph flipped us over with his assistant's help. The rush of cold water hit me like a slap in the face, the chest, the back—everywhere! Even though I couldn't swim anymore, it felt good to be in the water again.

Jessy was watching from the shore. He laughed and clapped when I pulled myself out of the water and onto the bottom of the overturned canoe.

By day I was struggling to master the physical process of canoeing on the ocean. By night I was struggling to learn the other part of Salish canoeing: the spiritual part.

This meant learning to sing the traditional Salish canoe songs to be used during departures and arrivals. And there were what they called the "Protocols." These were the activities that took place each time our canoe landed on the shores of another tribe. The Protocols involved introducing ourselves and our tribe to our hosts. They also included singing traditional songs and sharing stories of the day's journey.

It was like being an ambassador from one country who was visiting another country. Only this was about one tribal nation visiting another. To be courteous and respectful, we needed to ask permission to come ashore for a friendly visit.

I had been practicing with the canoe, learning the songs, and doing my physical therapy exercises. But others in the canoe family had also been busy. There was so much to do to get ready for this voyage.

Volunteers for the ground crew had to be rounded up. Maps and charts of the canoe route had to be plotted. Equipment, supplies, and food had to be gathered. On and on and on it went.

Most importantly, the canoe family had to make sure we had a motorized support boat to follow behind the canoe in case of emergencies. And the support boat's crew had to be with us for the entire two weeks of the trip.

Emmet George, one of the Duwamish members who lived in the area, ran a fishing company and owned several boats. He donated the use of his boat, called the Sockeye, for the support boat. Sockeye is a type of salmon that's important to the Salish people. Emmet also volunteered his own time to be the skipper of the boat. His two sons, who worked for him, would be helping out too. This made everyone in the canoe family really happy.

Billy and the carvers finished our canoe one week before our Tribal Journey was to begin. Everyone in the canoe family gathered for the dedication ceremony.

The finished canoe was bold and beautiful. The outside was painted black from front to back, top to bottom. On the bow, the image of a raven had been painted in red paint in the Northwest Coast Native style.

After a blessing prayer and song, Mr. Franks spoke. He said, "We're bringing back our old ways of doing things. These ways of thinking, talking, and living make up our Salish culture. Many of these things were not allowed by the American settlers when they took over our lives. Finally, in the past few years, we've taken back the freedom to do these things once again."

When the ceremony was over, everyone ate a traditional Salish meal. Fresh salmon was cooked on an open fire. It was served with wild blackberries and other edible wild foods. I'd never eaten some of these foods, and the tastes took a little getting used to.

"I'm really starting to see why these cultural lessons and activities are important," I said to Jessy as we ate. "You can't know who you are or where you came from without them."

"You think you understand it now," Jessy replied between bites, "but just wait till you live it for a few days. Just wait till you see dozens and dozens of canoes arriving on the final shore. And thousands of paddlers and supporters are all together singing the ancient songs and *living* the canoe culture. That, my friend, will blow you away.

Chapter 9
Whispers on the Wind

Departure day finally came. Hundreds of us gathered at Alki Beach for the launch at 7:00 a.m. There were paddlers, support team members, parents, and extended family. The tribal chairwoman was even there to give us words of encouragement. And a TV news crew. What a sight!

Mr. Franks offered a Native prayer for the journey ahead. Afterward, I gave Mom, Zak, and Shauna a good-bye hug. Mom was a little teary eyed. I sort of looked for Dad in the crowd. But of course, he wasn't there.

Our elders and others started singing a Salish canoe song. Within a few minutes everyone was singing, whether they knew the words or not.

Jessy wasn't going to be pulling during our first shift on the water. He lifted me out of my chair and carried me to the canoe. I settled into my seat and tightened the drawstring on my cedar hat so it wouldn't blow away.

"I'll see that this wheelchair makes it onto the support boat," Jessy said. "Your other chair is already in the van with all your camping gear."

Mrs. Anderson had been so proud to see me come out of my depression and take an active part in the whole canoe adventure. She had the hospital donate a second wheelchair for me. Two chairs allowed me to have one chair on the support boat and the other at our campsites. A land chair and a sea chair.

"Bet your land chair beats you to the first stop up at Suquamish." He laughed.

Of course my wheelchair would arrive at the first camp before the canoe would. That was the job of the ground support crew. They drove ahead during the day to set up camp at prearranged locations. That way our tents would already be up and ready when we arrived. And part of that crew would cook dinner for the paddlers. This allowed us to focus on pulling.

And pull we did. With Mr. Franks standing in the bow dressed in traditional Duwamish regalia, the Raven Canoe pushed away from shore. The lead puller set the pace as we stroked the water. Our skipper, steering from the rear, pointed us northward.

We left the singers and our families standing at the water's edge. As they became tiny specks on the horizon behind us, the adrenaline started pumping through my body. A moment of panic struck me unexpectedly. What had I been thinking? Was I crazy? It had been a nice fantasy, but I can't really do this! Can I?

Then, from behind us, a gust of wind came up. It was as though the energy of the singers on shore set the wind in motion. For a moment I thought I could hear those voices on that wind, even though I couldn't have really heard them.

But there was another sound within that wind. It was like a loud whisper. In a whoosh it said, "You can do this!" And right after hearing this message, I became aware of the sound of the paddles pushing through the water. Swoosh, swoosh, swoosh! And from within that sound came the same message, "You can do this!" And with every paddle stroke, I heard, "You can do this!"

At that moment, I remembered one of the talks Mr. Franks gave at a canoe family meeting. He said, "Don't be surprised if the spirit of Nature and the spirit of your Duwamish ancestors assist you in your journey. They are constantly present and available. All you have to do is tune in to them."

So I relaxed and went with the flow.

We pulled and sang with great energy that first morning. From time to time, one of our paddles kicked up a spray of cold water that misted over us. What a rush! Seagulls often drifted in the air nearby to check us out—such an unfamiliar sight we were.

Following their regular sailing schedules, ferryboats crossed behind us or in front of us. These huge vessels were loaded with cars, trucks, motorcycles, and pedestrians going to work or just heading from one of the islands to the mainland. In the greater Seattle area, ferries are as common as buses and commuter trains are in other cities.

As soon as someone on board a ferry noticed us, a group gathered on deck to snap photos or shoot a video on their cell phone. This happened several times as we made our way up through the waters of Puget Sound. We must've seemed like a blast from the past. A hundred years in the past.

After about four hours into the trip, the skipper called for a break. I was glad because my arms were about to give out. I signaled I was ready to take an extended rest. Using the walkie-talkie we had on the Raven, our skipper radioed the support boat. The Sockeye was several hundred feet away. It moved in beside us.

The support boat crew had come up with a way to get me out of the canoe easily. They used a device called a Lifesling. It had a padded, U-shaped loop attached to a long length of rope. They dropped the loop down to me. I slipped it around my back and under my arms.

A crew member on the Sockeye then turned a crank that slowly pulled me straight up from my canoe seat. Within a couple of minutes I was aboard the support boat. One of our backup pullers had climbed down the ladder into the canoe.

We had enough volunteer pullers to make up two full teams if needed. That way the canoe would be able to keep on schedule.

While we were stopped, sack lunches were also lowered into the canoe so everyone could eat.

"How was your first shift aboard the Raven?" Jessy asked as he steered my sea chair toward me. My own sack lunch was resting in the wheelchair seat.

"Absolutely amazing," I replied, eyeing the sack hungrily.

He started to lift me into the chair, but I stopped him. I rolled the wheelchair up beside me and tried to pull myself into the chair. My muscles were too tired and shaky from pulling all morning. I almost crashed to the deck.

Jessy grabbed the chair and steadied it. He then scooted me into the seat.

"Thanks," I said humbly. "I could do it if I wasn't so tired."

"I know you could," he said.

After fifteen minutes the lunch break was over. The support boat moved away from the canoe. We took up a position about a hundred yards away.

I watched the pullers as they continued the northward journey. It was an awesome sight. The log canoe, powered only by a group of determined people, crept along. It was so small when compared to the ocean and the coastline. It looked like a toothpick floating in a swimming pool.

During the afternoon, several other people switched from the support boat to the canoe. That way all of the pullers got to take part in the first day of the trip. In the late afternoon, we took another break. The Sockeye again slipped in beside the Raven.

Mr. Franks had been riding in the Sockeye. Now he spoke to everyone on both the support boat and the canoe.

"We are approaching the shores of our brothers, the Suquamish people. We will spend the night at their campground. But first we have to follow the canoe Protocols before we set foot on another tribal nation's land. Other canoes will be arriving from other tribes that are headed to Cowichan too. Each one follows the Protocols when it arrives. That means the Protocols will take awhile. So you have to be patient. Is everyone ready?"

As if with one voice, we jointly hollered, "Yes!"

I got to get back into the canoe for arrival at our first stop. So did Jessy. When we were close enough to see the Suquamish campgrounds, we began to sing our arrival song. A couple of other tribal canoes had already landed. A few more were coming in behind us.

These activities would be conducted every night we camped on another tribe's lands.

Mr. Franks stood up in the bow of the Raven. When we were close enough to be heard, he announced the name of our canoe, what tribe we were from, and who he was.

That was the first time I'd heard he was a direct descendent of Chief Seattle. That made him kind of like tribal royalty.

When he was finished with the proper announcements, he asked permission for us to come ashore to rest and feast. Permission was, of course, given.

We steered the Raven parallel to the shore. That's when I noticed my land chair sitting there waiting for me. Jessy must've read my mind. He jumped out of the canoe and ran to the chair.

Pulling the crutch out of the back pocket, he unfolded it and brought it to me. He then carried me to the shore. From there I hobbled toward our camp. Jessy pushed the empty wheelchair beside me.

But the ground was very uneven. That made it hard to walk with the crutch. Jessy saw the problem.

"What do you want to do," Jessy asked. "Walk or ride?"

"I want to drive," I said.

And with that, he turned the chair so I could slide into the seat. Folding the crutch, he placed it back in the chair's pocket. My muscles were sore, but I wanted to arrive at camp under my own power.

So I wheeled myself from the water's edge across a grassy area to the campground where our tents were waiting. Our ground crew had done a great job of setting up everything ahead of time.

Our hosts, members of the Suquamish Nation, greeted and welcomed us. A few people wanted to know all about how a kid in a wheelchair got to be a puller. I enjoyed telling a little of my story to the three or four people standing nearby.

The Suquamish people had prepared a wonderful feast for all the canoe guests who'd stopped there for the night. Singing and sharing went on for hours. But I was so exhausted, I had to make my way to my tent and my sleeping bag. I was so thankful for that ground crew.

I faded off to sleep with the sounds of laughter and Salish songs drifting across the camp.

Chapter 10
The Smell of the Ocean

Day two of the journey began early. We were up and at it by six o'clock. A cold fog had settled in overnight. I dressed in layers, knowing that I would warm up later. I could peel off the outer layers as the temperature climbed.

As I crawled out of the tent, my groggy brain protested. The voice in my head said, "Are you nuts? Go back to bed!" I tried to ignore it.

I dragged myself up into my waiting chair. My back and arm muscles were tight and sore. I slowly wheeled toward the campfire where the pullers were gathering.

The ground crew had cooked up eggs and bacon for us. They'd also put a cast-iron pot of coffee on the campfire. I needed something to kick-start the brain cells, so I got an empty mug and moved closer to the fire. This would be my first taste of something my parents drank every morning.

A member of the ground crew poured some of the thick black liquid into my outstretched cup. Steam rose from the mug, so I gave it a few minutes to cool down. I grabbed a plate of the hot food and found a picnic table to roll myself to.

The food was great. The coffee, on the other hand, was the worst tasting thing I'd ever put in my mouth. Next to liver.

I must've made a terrible face as I swallowed the caffeinated drink, because Jessy laughed at me as he sat down beside me. He had a plate of food and a cup of coffee, too.

"You look like you just took a bite of liver," he said.

"Is this the way coffee is supposed to taste?" I asked.

"No. You should've asked me about it first. I could've warned you." He took a big swig of his coffee.

"How can you drink it?" I asked.

"There are a lot of things you'll eat and drink if you're cold and hungry enough," he said. "You'll get used to it. It helps if you fill half the cup with that hazelnut-flavored cream over there."

"Now you tell me," I complained.

After breakfast, everyone in our camp gathered near the canoe to have a prayer for the day's journey.

"When you're out there on the water today, remember who you are," Mr. Franks said. "If you don't know who you are, this is the time and place to figure that out."

"How do we do that?" one of the young pullers asked.

"Pay attention to your surroundings. Listen to the birds and the splashing of the water. Smell the ocean and the forests nearby. Notice the warmth of the sun and the feel of the rain on your skin. Then close your eyes and go deep into your own mind to see what Spirit has waiting for you to discover."

That was heavy. Everyone was quiet for a few moments.

"And have fun!" he said as he ended his little talk with a smile.

With that, we scattered to begin performing our assigned tasks. The pullers either climbed into the canoe or onto the support boat. The ground crew began breaking down the camp and packing it up. We would see them at the next stop, on the Tulalip Reservation farther up the coast.

And so the daily pattern repeated itself. After an overnight stay at Tulalip, we pushed on to the Swinomish Reservation, the Samish Reservation, and then to Lummi. We shared stories, songs, and accounts of our trip at each stop. So did other canoe families.

And the number of canoes and people grew with each stop as more and more groups caught up with the tribal canoes coming from the south.

Each night we'd take a look at the maps and charts the canoe family had prepared. On the map you could see that tribal canoes were coming from the far northern regions of western Canada. Others were coming from farther south along the Washington State coast. Everyone's trip was timed so we'd all arrive on the same day on the shores of Cowichan Bay.

Chapter 11
Crossing the Straits

On the seventh morning of our journey I woke up on the Lummi Reservation. This tribal community was located on the northwest coast of Washington State. It was only about thirty miles from the Canadian border. But our final destination was located on Vancouver Island, a huge piece of land off the western coast of Canada.

So in order to get there, all the southern canoes had to cross the open waters of something called the Strait of Juan de Fuca.

"What's a strait?" I had asked Jessy before we left Seattle. I figured he'd know since he'd been on the last Tribal Journey.

"It's a narrow passage of water that connects two larger bodies of water," he'd answered. "This strait connects the Pacific Ocean to the Salish Sea."

"We have a sea named after us? That's cool!" I looked at the map Jessy had.

"What's a Juan de Fuca?" I followed up.

"That's a *who,* not a *what,*" he replied. "Juan de Fuca was some explorer who supposedly found this strait in the 1500s."

"Was it lost?" I asked.

"Ha-ha, very funny," Jessy said. "No, he found it for the Spaniards when they were exploring over here. We knew where it was all along."

"Oh." I nodded.

"Do you have any more dumb questions?" Jessy asked.

"As a matter of fact I do. When and where do we cross the borderline that separates the U.S. from Canada?"

"The international border between the two countries runs down the middle of the strait." He pointed to a small dotted line on the map.

"How do people know when they've crossed the border?" I asked. "Is there a line floating out in the water?"

"These *are* dumb questions," Jessy said. "Of course there's no line floating in the water. When we arrive at our first stop on Vancouver Island, we all have to show our passports."

"Now I get it. I was wondering when we'd need those."

"The Sockeye skipper will have all our passports locked in his safe on the support boat. Any more dumb questions?"

I thought for a minute. "No, not now, but I'm sure I'll have more dumb questions later."

So now we were pushing off the shores of the Lummi Nation, headed west. The morning was again cold and foggy.

I spent the morning shift on the Sockeye while other pullers had their turn on the Raven. I got to ride in the main cabin with the skipper, who was answering more of my dumb questions. How else is a fella going to learn anything?

The skipper had been watching the skies and listening to the weather reports for the area. He didn't like what he saw in either. The fog was not thinning out. The wind had picked up. The ocean's surface was choppy. The pullers were not getting very far and were exhausted.

"These are dangerous waters," the skipper said. "We're very close to the international shipping channel. That's where large freight carriers move shipping containers in and out of Vancouver. One of those monsters wouldn't see a little thirty-foot canoe in the fog."

So the skipper made a decision for safety's sake. He radioed the skipper of the Raven. He told them they needed to come aboard the Sockeye for the remainder of the morning. He'd tow the canoe as we crossed the stormy strait.

None of the pullers really wanted to get out. But Tribal Journey rules allowed canoes to be towed for short distances during bad weather or dangerous water conditions. After everyone was on board the Sockeye, the Raven was tied on behind. The skipper set off across the strait.

Meanwhile, fresh from the water, the pullers warmed themselves with blankets, coffee, and hot chocolate. I sat with them while they talked about how hard the going had been. As I listened, I noticed the fog getting even thicker. You could only see about thirty or forty feet in front of you.

All of a sudden a moving, rusty red wall broke through the fog and headed right for us. I didn't know what it could be. It scared me and I yelled.

"What's that thing coming right at us?"

Everyone turned to see the bow of a freighter ship as it became visible. It was barreling down on us. It must've been seven stories tall! The skipper saw it, too, and jumped into action.

"Hold on!" he commanded through the Sockeye's loudspeaker.

He punched the throttle at the same time he blasted the boat's horn. The Sockeye tilted backward as the engines cranked to full speed. I hadn't had time to grab anything to hold on to, so my wheelchair sped across the deck. I yelled again.

Luckily I was able to grab the handrail that surrounded the deck. That kept me from rolling to the stern and overboard. I held on as tight as I could.

Jessy saw what was happening and bolted across the deck to help me.

Our support boat easily moved out of the path of the freighter. But the Raven, being towed behind, just barely missed being hit. A huge wave crashed over the canoe, flipping it upside down. Of course, our paddles and spare life jackets were scattered in all directions.

Just as Jessy reached me on deck, the huge wave crashed into the side of the Sockeye. Our boat tipped sideways a little and then rolled back. The same wall of water hit Jessy and me full on. I had a firm grip on the handrail, but Jessy didn't.

The force of the water knocked him down and swept him toward the back of the boat. The stern had an opening in the handrail that allowed people to get on and off the deck. The water pushed him through that opening and into the ocean. Now Jessy was the one who needed help.

I spotted the Lifesling hanging on its rack not too far from me. That gizmo had been used daily to get me into and out of the canoe. It was time to use it for what it was designed to do—save someone who'd gone overboard.

The Sockeye was still rocking back and forth in the rough sea. But, wheeling my chair with an experienced hand, I was able to grab the Lifesling and head for the stern. We'd all learned how to use it. I first attached the rope to the crank. Then I flung the U-shaped loop out in the water toward Jessy.

He was just pulling himself up out of the water and onto the top of the overturned canoe. The water was very choppy. The canoe wobbled furiously in the turbulence. But he was able to hang on. Our trainer had been right: the canoe would float, no matter what.

"I'm all right," he shouted over the noise of the rolling sea. "I don't need the Lifesling."

The other pullers arrived at the stern to see what had happened to their beloved Raven.

They watched as Jessy examined the bottom of the canoe.

"I don't see any cracks or breaks in the hull," he shouted after a few minutes. "Who wants to help me flip it upright and gather up our paddles?"

A couple of the adult pullers jumped into the cold water. Each grabbed a life jacket from the water and put it on. Jessy got hold of one and put it on as well.

All three worked to turn the Raven over. Once the canoe was upright, they gathered up the scattered paddles and life jackets. Within a few minutes, all was back to normal. We used the Lifesling to get the three of them back on board the Sockeye.

And that ordeal served as our welcome to Canada. The rest of the trip was a piece of cake, as they say. We made three more overnight stops at Canadian Native communities. They were just as welcoming and friendly as the tribes south of the border.

But the closer we got to our final landing site, the more excited we all got. I heard from

Jessy and others who'd been on journeys before that the feeling you get is bigger than Christmas, your birthday, and graduation from school all rolled into one. That's big!

Chapter 12
Landing Day

The night before Landing Day we stayed with the people of the Malahat First Nations. In Canada, tribes are often called First Nations. The Malahat Reserve was about ten miles, as the canoe travels, from Cowichan's landing site.

The Cowichan canoe officials had decided to have canoes come into their shores in groups. These groups were defined by the direction they'd come from. The Duwamish canoe was part of the southern group. We'd all come from the Puget Sound area.

So, while we were camped at Malahat, all the southern canoe families held a meeting. We picked a time and place that we'd all gather before entering the landing area. That gathering place was about a mile from the landing site.

I really couldn't sleep much that night. The sounds of hundreds of pullers and ground crew members floated in the air until the wee hours of the morning. They were singing, and talking, even dancing. Were our tribal ancestors watching us? Were they as excited as we were about the coming day?

The clamor of pots and pans awoke me the next morning. It was still dark, but our valiant ground crew was up and at 'em. As I was struggling out of my tent, Mr. Franks came up to me.

"We wanted to wait until this morning to tell you," he said.

"Tell me what?" Did I miss something?

"The family has voted to have you ride in the bow of the canoe when we arrive." He was smiling a big grin.

"But that's *your* place," I protested.

"I'll be right behind you," he replied. "But you've been an inspiration to all of us. You have some surprising gifts given to you by the Creator."

"A few things *have* happened that really surprised me," I admitted.

"I think the surprises in your life are just beginning," he said. "Anyway, we're proud to call you a member of the Raven Canoe Family."

"I don't know what to say," I said.

"Just say yes."

"Yes." I repeated.

"Good. I have some regalia for you to wear. We'll have it on the support boat. You can ride there this morning. Later, we'll put you in the canoe."

"Thank you, Mr. Franks."

"Have some breakfast. I'll see you on board the Sockeye." He headed back to the main group as Jessy stepped up.

"I'm here to help you with anything you need today," he said.

"Really?"

"You're like a dignitary today. That's why you're riding in the front."

"Okay then," I said. I wanted to take full advantage of the situation. "I'll have pancakes, maple syrup, and hot chocolate with whipped cream. On the double!"

"Don't push it," Jessy said with a laugh. I laughed too.

It turned out to be a calm day out on the water. The sun was shining. A slight breeze cooled the air. The pullers were quiet for the most part. After two weeks of hard work, sometimes in dangerous conditions, everyone was thinking about the journey. We all had mixed emotions: both glad and sad that it was coming to an end.

As the Raven approached the gathering place for the southern canoes, it slowed. The Sockeye pulled in beside it so I could be lowered into the front seat. I'd put on the regalia Mr. Franks had for me. It included a red and blue blanket with small shells sewn all over it. And there was a cedar branch wreath that went on top of my cedar hat.

Mr. Franks, also dressed in his regalia, took the seat behind me.

When all the southern canoes were ready, we began pulling the last mile of our journey. We formed a single line of about twenty-five canoes.

As we neared Cowichan Bay, we began to see the clusters of canoes from the other directions—the north, east, and west. I was startled as I began to understand the grand size of the whole scene. How many canoes were there?

Our skipper signaled that it was time for us to start our arrival song. We'd practiced this many times along the way. Our paddles stroked the water in sync with the song. Other canoes began their arrival songs as well.

The Raven was about in the middle of the line of southern canoes as we approached the shores of the Cowichan First Nation. Again I was startled to see the size of this event. There must've been five thousand people lining the shore. They were clapping, singing, hollering, whistling—you name it.

The southern canoes circled past the main area where the Cowichan leaders and elders stood on a raised platform. In front of the platform, closer to the water, was a large group of singers who belted out a Salish honoring song. Several used hand drums to pound out the beat of the song.

Mr. Franks helped me to stand in the bow of the Raven. Leaning on my aluminum crutch, I stood as proudly as my broken body would allow.

I sang our arrival song as loudly as I could. In that moment I felt the power and emotion of thousands of people all focused on one joyful celebration. We were all celebrating what was once banned. We were celebrating the rebirth of our identity as Salish people, the rebirth of our ancient culture.

I'm embarrassed to admit that tears rolled down my cheeks as this feeling overwhelmed me. I quickly recovered my cool and dried my eyes, hoping that no one had noticed.

The only word I could think of to describe what was happening was "spectacle." This was certainly a spectacle. Several TV news crews were filming the event. Many personal cameras also recorded the arrivals.

An M.C. on shore described the scene over loud speakers. "Canoes have been coming into the bay for quite some time now. More are coming. I can't see the end of the line. Can anyone see the end?"

The canoes from the east were the first ones invited to come to shore. Ten or twelve canoes from that group lined up side by side in the water. As a unit, they moved toward the shore until their bows touched land. One by one, a dignitary from each canoe introduced the canoe and announced where the people in it were from.

The chairman of the Cowichan tribe welcomed each canoe to their shores. All were invited to come ashore for feasting and Protocols. As soon as one line of canoes finished, another line of ten or twelve pulled in beside them.

While these canoes were performing their arrival duties, other canoes continued to enter the bay and circle the area.

Finally, it came time for the southern canoes to approach the shore. Our group lined up side by side and drifted in. I was still leaning on my crutch, with Mr. Franks standing behind me.

Our turn came. "Mr. Chairman, we are the Raven Canoe from the proud Duwamish Nation," Mr. Franks announced. "We are members of the Raven Canoe Family. Standing in our bow is a young Duwamish man of great courage, Jason Morgan. He overcame many obstacles to be a part of this journey. We present him to you as our most outstanding member. We are honored by your invitation to come to your shores. We have traveled more than two hundred miles."

The Cowichan chairman spoke. "Mr. Franks, this young man needs no introduction to us. His story has traveled ahead of you. It has become almost a legend among the people of the canoe. We are honored to have you come to our shores."

Mr. Franks proudly patted me on the shoulder. I was speechless. I sat down to rest.

After all the canoes had lined the shores and performed their arrival ceremonies, an honor song began among the northern canoes. They used the handles of their paddles to pound out the rhythm on the floor of their canoes.

The song and the beat spread to all the canoes. It then spread across the shoreline like a wildfire spreading across a field of grass. As the sound grew, a kind of tingling spread through my body. I didn't know what it was. I was vibrating from head to foot.

To my surprise, I even felt it in my dead leg. For the first time since my accident, I felt something in that leg. It didn't last long, and the effect wasn't permanent. But that brief experience gave me new hope.

When the song ended, the M.C. said, "We've done a count and there are 109 tribal canoes here today. Can you believe it?"

The crowd roared, clapped, and cheered even louder than before.

The M.C. invited all the canoe families to participate in the Protocols that would begin at the tribe's headquarters that evening. We all turned our canoes and headed across the bay to a beach where we could disembark.

Buses took all the pullers to the tribal park where our camps had already been set up by our hard-working ground crews. My first order of business: a nap.

That evening, the Cowichan volunteers had set up dinner for us in the tribe's gym. Pullers and ground crews lined up and filed inside to get plates of delicious Native foods. I had never seen such a spread of unusual things to eat, so I had to ask the servers what some of it was.

One large pot held something called stinging nettle and elk stew. Another held cooked greens made from fern tops. Moving down the line, there were clams, crabs, eels, and wild bird eggs.

Smacking his lips, Jessy piled his plate high with large helpings of the stuff. So I did the brave thing and filled my plate as well. Over the teeth, past the gums, look out stomach, here it comes.

The final food station was a sort of cobbler made of wild blackberries, huckleberries, and raspberries. That looked really good!

Surprisingly, most of food tasted terrific. The dessert was the best I'd ever had. I was so hungry, I cleaned my plate.

Afterward, Protocols began. A large central canopy had been set up at the edge of a mowed field. Several other canopies formed a large U shape around a central grassy field.

I heard that it would require four days of Protocols to allow all 109 canoe families to share their stories, songs, and thanks.

Jessy and I sat with our canoe family under a large canopy. Though I was in my wheelchair, I also had my folding crutch at hand.

The same M.C. who had done all of the announcing at the landing was on the microphone. "Before we go any further with Protocols tonight, we have to do something else first."

A hush fell over the crowd.

"Everyone here has heard about the kid in the wheelchair."

Uh-oh, what was this, I wondered.

"We all want to meet him and hear his story. So without any further delay, we ask Jason from the Raven Canoe Family to come up."

The applause was loud. Jessy and the rest of my canoe family urged me forward. Jessy started pushing me toward the announcer's canopy. People continued to applaud.

Halfway to the microphone, I put both my feet on the ground.

"What's going on, buddy?" Jessy asked.

Without saying anything, I pulled out my crutch and unfolded it.

"I want to try walking," I said. Jessy came around to the front of the chair to help me up. I waved him off.

Realizing what was going on, the crowd grew quiet.

I planted the crutch firmly on the ground in front of me. With all my strength, I pulled myself up to a standing position. The crowd went wild!

I hobbled the rest of the way to the microphone—on my own. Jessy just watched and smiled.

When I arrived at the microphone, the M.C. shook my hand and stepped away. I turned to face the audience. Again I was startled to see the size of the gathering.

Since I wasn't used to speaking in front a group of people, my first words were weak and shaky. I started again. My thoughts flashed back to spring break. It seemed so long ago.

I told them about my car wreck and my recovery. And about my introduction to canoe carving, my introduction to canoe culture, and the warm welcome I'd received from the Raven Canoe Family. As I spoke it out loud, I realized how grateful I was to have experienced it all.

I learned so much about myself during this Tribal Journey. It had really been a personal tribal journey. I had found a meaningful place in the mad, crazy rush of everyday life. And I'd found a new sense of courage.

When I finished talking, a Salish song began somewhere in the crowd. People stood up from their seats and joined in the song. A couple of people stepped out into the open field with their hands raised. With palms up, elbows bent, they moved their arms to the beat of the song in the traditional Salish gesture of thanks.

They began to circle the field as they sang. Soon others joined in the circle. One of the Cowichan elders approached me at the microphone. With Jessy's help, the old man led me to the center of the growing circle. It wasn't long before every able-bodied person in that arena was dancing in the circle.

That did it. Tears welled up in my eyes. What an awesome ending to my first Tribal Journey. What an awesome beginning to my own personal tribal journey.

A new sense of strength flowed through my body. A new sense of determination flowed through my mind. I *would* walk again, no matter how long it took. I *would* swim again too.

Until then, I was proud to know I was a Coast Salish Indian. A member of the Raven Canoe Family. A part of the ancient Duwamish Nation.

About the Author

Gary Robinson, a writer and filmmaker of Cherokee and Choctaw Indian descent, has spent more than twenty-five years working with American Indian communities to tell the historical and contemporary stories of Native people in all forms of media.

His television work has aired on PBS, Turner Broadcasting, Ovation Network, and others. His nonfiction books, *From Warriors to Soldiers* and *The Language of Victory*, reveal little-known aspects of American Indian service in the U.S. military from the Revolutionary War to modern times. In addition to *Tribal Journey*, he has also written another novel, *Thunder on the Plains,* and two children's books that share aspects of Native American culture through popular holiday themes: *Native American Night Before Christmas* and *Native American Twelve Days of Christmas*. He lives in rural central California.

7th Generation *publications celebrate the stories and achievements of Native people in North America through fiction and biography.*

For more information, visit:
nativevoicesbooks.com

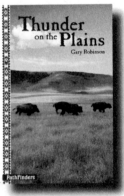

Thunder on the Plains
Gary Robinson
978-1-939053-00-8
$9.95

A Native teen deals with the loss of his father by attending a summer survival camp. After two years, Danny Wind is still not over his father's death. And when his mom marries a white man and they move to a new "white bread" neighborhood, Danny's life gets even worse. The school principal considers him a troublemaker and he has to avoid Willy, a bully who calls him "redskin" and "Tonto." After he acts out and gets suspended from school, Danny's mom decides to send him to a summer survival camp for American Indian teens.

Danny is sure he is in for a terrifically boring summer—there isn't even Internet access on the reservation. Instead he meets other Indian kids, learns to ride and care for horses, and develops a relationship with his grandfather, who teaches him the ways of his people.

Before long, Danny decides that life on the reservation is pretty cool. But never in his craziest dreams did he expect to become involved in rescuing bison from Yellowstone National Park—much less planning the adventurous mission!

Available from your local bookstore or you can buy them directly from:

Book Publishing Company • P.O. Box 99 • Summertown, TN 38483
1-800-695-2241

Please include $3.95 per book for shipping and handling.